Written by
James Gelsey

A
LITTLE APPLE
PAPERBACK

SCHOLASTIC INC.
New York Toronto London Auckland Sydney
Mexico City New Delhi Hong Kong Buenos Aires

For Jake and Josh

ISBN 0-439-42072-5

Copyright © 2002 by Hanna-Barbera.
SCOOBY-DOO and all related characters and elements
are trademarks of and © Hanna-Barbera.
CARTOON NETWORK and logo are trademarks of and
© Cartoon Network.
(s02)
Published by Scholastic Inc. All rights reserved.
SCHOLASTIC, LITTLE APPLE, and associated logos are
trademarks and/or registered trademarks of Scholastic Inc.

Designed by Carisa Swenson

12 11 10 9 8 7 6   5 6 7/0

Special thanks to Duendes del Sur for cover and interior illustrations.
Printed in the U.S.A.
First printing, December 2002

Chapter 1

The Mystery Machine cruised down a winding, tree-lined road with Fred behind the wheel. Shaggy and Scooby-Doo were asleep in the back, snoring very loudly.

"Sounds like Shaggy and Scooby enjoyed the camping trip," Velma said, studying the road map.

"I'll say," Daphne agreed. "There's something about being outdoors that helps you relax and forget all your troubles."

"The only troubles Shaggy and Scooby have are figuring out when their next meal is going to be," Fred joked.

As the three of them laughed, something darted out of the woods. Fred slammed on the brakes, jolting Shaggy and Scooby awake.

"Hey, like, what's the big idea, Fred?" Shaggy asked. He yawned and slowly sat up. "I was dreaming about a giant pizza."

"Forget about the pizza," Daphne said. "Check that out!"

A large black horse stood in the middle of the road. A cloaked figure sat in the saddle. The rider flicked the reins, and the horse be-

gan galloping straight at the Mystery Machine. The rider's long purple cape flowed in the wind.

"I sure hope he can see us with that hood pulled down over his face," Daphne said.

Scooby-Doo sat up yawning as the horse stopped right in front of the van.

"Ruh? Rhat's rat?" Scooby asked, looking out the windshield.

"Beware the Ruppscupper curse!" the mysterious horseback rider hissed. The rider flipped back its hood, revealing a ghostly, glowing green head. And then it lifted its head off its shoulders!

"Zoinks!" Shaggy exclaimed.

"Jinkies!" Velma cried.

"Rikes!" Scooby barked. "Ri'm roing rack ro reep!" He dived down and tried to hide under Shaggy.

The horseback rider raised its head high into the air.

"Turn back now and avoid Forest City!"

3

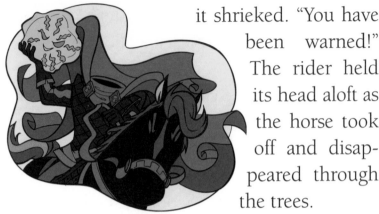

it shrieked. "You have been warned!" The rider held its head aloft as the horse took off and disappeared through the trees.

"What was that?" Daphne asked.

"If I didn't know better, I'd say it was the headless horseman," Velma said.

"But that's just a story," Fred said. "Besides, what would it be doing here?"

"Like, telling us to avoid Forest City," Shaggy said. "Weren't you paying attention? And believe me, that's not a warning I need to hear twice. So let's just get the van in gear and get out of here."

"Shaggy's right," Velma said with a nod.

"He is?" Daphne asked.

"I am?" Shaggy said.

Fred nodded back. "Yup. We should get

going." Fred put the van back into gear and started driving again.

Shaggy breathed a sigh of relief.

"After all, we'll never make it to Forest City to investigate this mystery if we don't get going," Velma added.

"Me and my big mouth," moaned Shaggy. He looked down at Scooby-Doo. "Come on, Scooby, you don't have to pretend to be asleep anymore. It's gone now."

Scooby slowly opened his left eye and looked around. Then he opened his right eye. Then he sat up and checked things out again.

"Rhew!" he said.

The Mystery Machine sped past a large sign.

"'Welcome to Forest City!'" Daphne read. "'Home of the Friendliest Trees Around.'"

"And spookiest horseback riders," Shaggy whispered to Scooby.

As the van rounded a big bend in the road, the gang noticed a small log cabin at the edge of the forest. Some cars were parked in front of the cabin, and there was a small crowd of people milling around.

"Let's take a look," Fred said. "Maybe someone saw the headless horseman come this way."

"I have to admit it's a little strange to see a log cabin nowadays," Daphne said. "I wonder who lives there."

Fred steered the van into the parking area and turned off the engine. The gang got out and looked around. As they did, a gust of wind blew a yellow piece of paper against Shaggy's shirt.

"'Ground-breaking ceremony today,'" Velma read. "'Future site of the Chow 'n' Chew Restaurant, home of the Chow 'n' Chew Chomper.'"

"Like, did you say Chow 'n' Chew Chomper?" Shaggy asked.

Scooby licked his lips.

"Sorry, fellas, but it'll be several months before they open the restaurant," a voice said from behind them. "But don't worry, it'll be worth the wait!"

Chapter 2

The gang turned around and faced a short man in a blue suit.

"I'm Walt Sturgeon, Mr. Chow 'n' Chew himself," the man said.

"Excuse me, Mr. Sturgeon, but are you really going to build a restaurant here?" asked Daphne.

"You bet, young lady," said an elderly man as he walked over. He wore brown pants held up with suspenders and a yellow shirt. "Just as soon as we can get the cabin moved downtown to the Forest City Museum."

8

"You're going to move this entire cabin?" asked Velma.

"You bet," the man said. "This cabin's over a hundred years old. It's an historic landmark. If you think I'd let people tear down a piece of Forest City history for a fast-food restaurant, you don't know me very well."

"Actually, sir, we don't know you at all," Daphne said.

The man laughed. "Of course you don't," he said. "I'm Happy Higgenbotham. And this is where Forest City's founding father first settled in 1879. I've been the caretaker of the Jedidiah Ruppscupper homestead for more than fifty years."

Shaggy's eyes widened in horror. "R-r-r-ruppscupper?" he stammered.

"As in the Ruppscupper curse?" Daphne added.

"Curse? What Ruppscupper curse?" Walt Sturgeon asked. "Happy, what's this all about?"

"Oh, nothing, Walt," Happy said. "Hey, I

9

saw some reporters behind the house. They were asking for you before. Why don't you go talk to them while I get every-thing ready for the ground-breaking?"

"Fine idea," Walt Sturgeon said as he marched away.

Once Walt Sturgeon was out of earshot, Happy turned back to the gang. "Where'd you kids hear about the Ruppscupper curse?" he asked.

"From the headless horseman," Shaggy blurted out.

"You kids saw a headless horseman?" Happy asked.

"A few miles up the road," Fred replied.

10

"It darted out from the woods, told us to avoid Forest City, and then disappeared back into the trees."

"After it took off its head," Shaggy said.

"If you don't mind my saying so," Daphne began, "you're suddenly not looking very happy, Happy."

Happy Higgenbotham scratched his head and frowned. He looked around to make sure no one else was listening.

"Listen, kids," he whispered. "There's an old story about Jedidiah Ruppscupper. The story goes that after Jed decided to build a town here, some unsavory folks tried to scare him off the land. Local folklore says that one night a headless horseman chased Jed into the forest. No one ever saw Jed or the headless horseman again."

"Until today," Fred added.

Happy nodded slowly. "I gotta tell ya, kids, I don't have a good feeling about this," he said. "But do me a favor — don't say anything to Mr. Sturgeon. I need his help to save the log cabin. If he pulls out, all of this history will be lost forever."

"Maybe you should have thought about that before making a deal with Walt Sturgeon!" another voice exclaimed.

Everyone looked up and saw a man with a pinched expression on his face. His red-and-black bow tie jiggled every time he spoke.

"I thought we had a verbal understanding to pursue an oral agreement, Happy Higgenbotham!" the man said rather loudly. "Then I read about the ground-breaking in today's paper!" The man waved the newspaper in Happy's face.

Happy waved his hands at the man. "Shh-hhhhhhhh! Not so loud, Cullen," Happy said. "We had no such thing. We had a friendly conversation, and you said you'd get back to me and you never did."

The man opened his mouth to respond, but then noticed the gang standing there. "Excuse me?"

"Sorry, Cullen," Happy said. "These young people are acquaintances of mine. We've got . . . er . . . um . . . a mutual friend."

"You're going to need all your friends, Happy," Cullen said. "Because I'm about to become your biggest enemy. You know I've had my eye on this land for a new Jolly Roger's Seafood Buffet."

Shaggy's and Scooby's eyes lit up.

"Jolly Roger's Seafood Buffet?" asked Shaggy. "Like, that's one of our favorite restaurants."

"Cullen Gasket owns the local Jolly Roger's franchise," Happy explained. Then he turned to Cullen Gasket. "I'm sorry, Cullen, but Mr. Sturgeon offered to help me preserve the cabin. My first loyalty has to be to the memory of Jedidiah Ruppscupper."

"Curse you, Happy Higgenbotham, curse that Jedidiah Ruppscupper, and curse the Chow 'n' Chew!" Cullen replied. He stormed off.

"Cover your ears, Scooby," Shaggy said. "That man just insulted one of our other favorite restaurants."

"I'm sure Mr. Gasket will get over it," Velma said. "After all, it's only a restaurant."

"To you and me, maybe," Happy replied. "But not to him."

Chapter 3

appy Higgenbotham and the gang walked up to the front of the log cabin. Happy stepped onto the front porch and knocked on the knotted-pine logs.

"Solid as the day it was built," he said proudly. "Jed Ruppscupper built this cabin with his own two hands. Took him almost a year to cut down the trees and put it all together."

As they admired the cabin's craftsmanship, the sound of hoofbeats filled the air.

"Rikes!" Scooby barked. "Readress rorseran!" He jumped into Shaggy's arms.

"Relax, Scooby," Velma said. "That sounds like two horses to me. And I doubt there are two headless horsemen."

"Probably just the Kibble sisters. Sadie and Katie Kibble own a horse farm just beyond that row of trees behind the cabin," Happy said. "If you don't mind, I'm going to excuse myself to get things ready for the ceremony. Feel free to look around."

The gang walked around to the back of the cabin. A woman in a brown tweed jacket and black riding pants stood next to her horse. She reached into her pocket and took out a handful of something. She opened her palm and offered it to the horse, who eagerly devoured the snacks.

"Those are beautiful horses," Daphne called, walking over to them. "May I pet one?"

"You can pet mine," said the woman in the brown jacket. Her horse was dark brown

with a yellow mane. "Cocoa here doesn't mind strangers."

"Thunder isn't too crazy about them," the other woman said from atop her horse. She wore a bright red windbreaker and blue jeans. Her horse was light brown with a dark brown mane and tail.

Daphne walked up to Cocoa and gently stroked the horse's neck.

"My name is Daphne," she said. "And

these are my friends Fred, Velma, Shaggy, and Scooby-Doo."

"I'm Sadie," the woman in brown said. "And that's my sister, Katie."

"Happy Higgenbotham tells us you own a horse farm back there," Fred said.

"Happy Higgenbotham should mind his own business!" Katie said.

"Manners, Katie," Sadie said.

"I'm sorry, but I'm hopping mad at that Happy Higgenbotham," Katie said. She took a folded newspaper article from her windbreaker pocket. "We had to find out in the newspaper that a fast-food restaurant is being built here. Do you have any idea how upsetting that will be to the horses?"

"Like, they don't like fast food?" asked Shaggy.

"No, Shaggy, I think Ms. Kibble is upset because the traffic and people will disturb the horses," Velma said.

"Some of our horses are very high-strung," Sadie explained. "The least little thing can set them off. Three times in the past month alone, one of our horses kicked its way out of its stall and ran away."

"How did you get it back?" asked Daphne.

"Fortunately, we have a very sophisticated way of tracking our horses," Sadie said. "So we were able to follow its trail."

"But that's not the point," Katie said. "The point is that Happy Higgenbotham at least owed us the courtesy of an explanation before any decisions were made. Now he's left us with very few options."

Sadie sent Katie a stern look. But before Katie could respond, Scooby's voice pierced the silence. "Reeeeeeeelp!"

19

Fred, Daphne, and Velma looked around and realized Shaggy and Scooby were gone.

"Scooby-Doo! Where are you?" Daphne called.

"Rover rere!" Scooby replied.

Fred, Daphne, and Velma followed Scooby's voice around the other side of the cabin. There they saw Shaggy standing next to an old-fashioned well pump. A trickle of water dripped from the spout and then stopped. Scooby sat against a tall pine tree about fifty feet away. He was soaking wet.

"What happened?" asked Fred.

"Like, Scooby wanted a drink of water from this water fountain," Shaggy explained. "So I said I'd hold the handle while he took a sip. I started pumping but nothing happened. Scooby got in for a closer look and then the water shot out — and blew Scooby clear across the yard!"

"That's not a water fountain, Shaggy," Velma said. "It's a water pump. There's a well beneath the ground. This is where Jedidiah Ruppscupper got his water."

"Next time, be more careful," Fred said. "The last thing we need is for the two of you to cause any trouble."

"If there's one thing you can count on, Fred-eroony," Shaggy replied, "it's for Scoob and me to stay out of trouble."

21

The gang walked around to the front of the cabin. A small crowd was gathering on the grass. Out in the parking area, Fred noticed someone else on horseback riding toward the cabin.

"I wonder who that is," he said.

"The way he's riding, he looks like a real cowboy," Velma said.

The gang watched the horseback rider guide his horse onto the grass and up to the front of the cabin. He dismounted and carefully tied the reins to the porch railing. The rider wore brown pants and a denim shirt, with a red bandanna around his neck. He walked up to Walt Sturgeon.

"Where's Happy Higgenbotham?" the man asked.

"Who may I say is asking?" Walt said.

"Rudy Rupper," the man said.

"In that case, I have no idea," Walt said. "Now if you'll excuse me, we're about to conduct a very important ceremony." Walt turned away from Rudy Rupper and studied his short speech for the ceremony.

Rudy Rupper scanned the crowd with his eyes. When he heard the log cabin door open, he spun around.

Happy Higgenbotham stepped out of the cabin. His eyes widened when he saw Rudy Rupper.

"Happy Higgenbotham," the man announced. "I've got a bone to pick with you."

"Rudy? Rudy Ruppscupper?" Happy said. "Where have you been? I've been looking for you for six years!"

"Well, you found me," Rudy said.

"I thought you said your name was Rudy Rupper," Walt Sturgeon interrupted.

"I've been riding my way across the United States and Europe for the past six years," Rudy said. "My name got too heavy to carry along, so I shortened it."

"What brings you back here, Rudy?" Happy asked.

"This!" Rudy said, thrusting his hand into his coat pocket. He took out a handful of horse snacks. "Sorry, wrong pocket." He reached into the other pocket and took out a newspaper. "I've been back one day and the first thing I see is this article describing how you're about to turn my great-great-great-

grandpappy's home into some kind of Chewing Chump restaurant."

"That's Chow 'n' Chew," Walt said.

"I'm sorry, Rudy," Happy said. "Like I said, I tried to find you. But you were impossible to reach. Plus, you changed your name. Besides, you know as well as I do that as caretaker of your great-great-great-grandfather's homestead, I have complete authority to take whatever steps I see fit to preserve it."

Rudy Rupper stared at Happy Higgenbotham.

"Do you think there's going to be a gunfight?" Shaggy whispered.

"That only happens in Westerns, Shaggy," Daphne said. "People today don't have gunfights anymore."

"Mark my words, Happy Higgenbotham," Rudy warned. "If my great-great-great-grandpappy were alive today, he'd never let you get away with this."

Without another word, Rudy Rupper walked over to his horse. He untied the reins and climbed into the saddle. With a gentle flick of the reins, the horse turned and walked slowly back toward the road.

Walt Sturgeon ran up to Happy. "What is going on here, Happy?" he asked nervously. "Are you sure everything is all right?"

Happy smiled. "Listen, Mr. Sturgeon, both of our attorneys have made sure all the paperwork is in order," he said. "We can't let these crazy people stand in our way."

"You're right," Walt Sturgeon agreed. "Let's break some ground for Ruppscupper's Chow 'n' Chew!"

Chapter 5

red, Daphne, Velma, Shaggy, and Scooby joined the small crowd in front of the cabin. Walt Sturgeon stood on the porch. Happy Higgenbotham stood next to him, holding two shovels.

"Welcome, friends," Walt Sturgeon began. "Over one hundred years ago, Forest City's founding father built this cabin as his home."

As Walt spoke, some of the reporters took his picture, while others scribbled in their notebooks.

"Today I am pleased to announce that the Chow 'n' Chew Corporation will help preserve this historic monument by moving it to the Forest City Museum," Walt continued. "In its place will rise a new tribute to Jed Ruppscupper's vision for Forest City: Ruppscupper's Chow 'n' Chew."

"Like, I hope they fix that water fountain before it opens," Shaggy whispered to Scooby. "Otherwise they're in for some soggy Chompers."

He and Scooby giggled.

"Shhh!" Daphne said.

"And in the spirit of the partnership between the past and the future, I've asked Happy Higgenbotham to join me in this historic ground-breaking," Walt announced.

Walt and Happy stepped off the porch and walked over to the middle of the front yard. The two men stood next to each other.

"To the past!" Happy proclaimed, sinking his shovel into the ground.

"To the future!" Walt echoed, also sticking his shovel into the dirt.

The sound of hoofbeats suddenly filled the air.

"Must be the Kibble sisters," Velma said.

"Or maybe Rudy Rupper changed his mind," Daphne said.

The hoofbeats continued to get louder until something burst out from behind the trees.

"Zoinks! It's the headless horseman!" Shaggy exclaimed.

"Rikes!" Scooby cried.

The black-cloaked figure galloped around the crowd three times before coming to a stop. The black horse reared up on its back legs.

"I command you to leave this land at once and never return!" the horseman commanded. "Disobey me and you will meet the fate of Jedidiah Ruppscupper!"

Walt Sturgeon dropped his shovel and ran toward the cabin.

"Freeze!" the horseman shouted.

Walt stopped in his tracks.

"I've got a special present for you, Chow-boy." The horseman laughed and threw back its hood, revealing the same glowing green head the gang had seen before.

"Man, don't take off your head, don't take off your head, don't take off your head," Shaggy whispered.

The horseman reached up with both hands and lifted its head from its shoulders.

"It took off its head," Shaggy moaned.

"CATCH!" the horseman said as it tossed its head to Walt. The horseman galloped around the side of the cabin and disappeared back into the woods.

Walt caught the head and looked down at its angry, glowing eyes and spooky green mouth.

"Ahhhhhhh!" he shrieked, tossing the head away. It sailed through the air and

Happy reflexively caught it. He, too, glanced at the frightening face and tossed the head away. This time, it sailed over to Scooby, who watched the glowing head land on the ground in front of him with a *SPLAT!*

"Where are you going, Mr. Sturgeon?" Happy asked.

"Forget the paperwork, Happy," Walt called, marching toward the parking area. "As long as there's a headless horseman riding around here, our deal is off!"

"But wait!" Happy shouted. "Without you, who'll save the cabin? Please come back, Mr. Sturgeon!"

While Happy ran after Walt Sturgeon, Fred consulted with the others.

"Well, gang, it looks to me like we've got a genuine mystery on our hands," he said.

"And I think some of it got on my shoes, too," Shaggy added. He shook the goopy remains of the horseman's splattered head from his sneakers.

Chapter 6

The gang studied the goopy, dissolving mess that used to be the horseman's head. Scooby gave it a careful sniff. He sniffed some more and tried to figure out why the smell was so familiar.

"What is it, Scoob?" asked Shaggy.

"Rell-O," Scooby said.

"Jell-O?" Fred asked.

"Of course," Velma said. "It's merely lime gelatin that was made in a head-shaped mold. I'll bet if we look hard enough we'll find a tiny light that made it look like it was glowing."

"Velma's right," Daphne said. "Look." She

35

reached down and picked up a miniature flashlight.

"Let me see that a minute, Daph," Shaggy said. He took the flashlight from her and gave it a lick. "Yup, lime all right. Good work, Velma. Now that the mystery's solved, what do you say we all go home?"

"Hold on there, Shaggy," Fred said. "We've only just started to solve the mystery. We've still got to find some more clues if we're going to help Happy Higginbotham save the cabin."

"Fred's right," Daphne agreed. "And the quickest way to do that is to split up."

"I'll take Shaggy and Scooby with me into the woods," Velma said. "The horseman may have left some clues behind."

"Great," Fred said. "Daphne and I will look around here some more and then join you."

Velma, Shaggy, and Scooby walked toward the row of trees alongside and behind the cabin.

"I think the horseman came through around here," Velma said. She scanned the area for signs of recent movement. "Aha, there's the path. Come on."

"I don't know about this, Velma," Shaggy said. "I remember reading somewhere about this girl who wandered into the woods and the next thing she knew, a big, bad wolf was after her and her grandmother."

Velma rolled her eyes. "That's Little Red Riding Hood, Shaggy. Now let's concentrate on finding clues."

After only a few steps into the woods, Velma, Shaggy, and Scooby were surrounded by tall pine trees.

"We're definitely on the right path,"

Velma said. "Look what I just found." She showed Shaggy and Scooby a torn piece of newspaper.

"Maybe one of the squirrels was reading the comics?" Shaggy suggested.

"It's a piece of the newspaper article about today's ceremony," Velma reported. "I'm going to show this to Fred and Daphne. You two keep looking. I'll be right back."

Velma walked down the path back to the cabin.

"Well, pal, I guess it's just you and me," Shaggy said.

"Rand ruh rig, rad rolf," Scooby joked.

"My, what big ears you have," Shaggy said.

"Retter ro rear rou rith," Scooby answered.

"Speaking of hearing," Shaggy said, "do you hear that?"

Scooby perked up his ears. A rustling sound came from behind a large log.

"It's coming from over there," Shaggy said. "Behind that log."

Shaggy and Scooby ran behind a tree and peeked out.

"What do you think it is?" Shaggy asked.

"Rig, rad rolf?" Scooby suggested.

"Like, right now I'd give anything for it to be the big, bad wolf," Shaggy said. "And not some creepy horseback rider with a squishy green head."

The sound grew louder, and Shaggy and Scooby jumped back behind the tree.

"Don't move, Scooby, and close your eyes," Shaggy whispered. "Maybe if we can't see it, it won't see us."

They shut their eyes and the sound got louder. Shaggy very carefully opened his right eye just a sliver. It was open just enough for him to see something standing next to them.

"Relax, Scooby, it's just a squirrel," Shaggy said, exhaling deeply.

As soon as Shaggy and Scooby moved,

the squirrel darted away. "I wonder what it was doing behind that log?" Shaggy said.

They walked over and looked behind the log. There they saw a pile of oats and nut clusters.

"Like, look at this, Scoob," Shaggy said. "Genuine trail mix!"

They each grabbed a handful and started munching.

"I never knew this stuff really grew on trails," Shaggy said.

"Ree, reither," Scooby agreed.

As they turned around to head back to the cabin, they heard another rustling sound come from across the path.

"I guess that squirrel's back for more," Shaggy said. "Come on out, little buddy, there's still plenty!"

But this time it wasn't the squirrel.

"Headless horseman!" Shaggy cried. "Let's get out of here, Scooby-Doo!"

Chapter 7

Shaggy and Scooby ran down the forest path with the headless horseman in pursuit. They burst through the trees and ran behind the cabin. The headless horseman galloped after them, splattering mud on the side of the cabin when it ran past the water pump.

Shaggy and Scooby ran through the cabin's back door. They slammed it shut and stood with their backs against it. The cabin was one big room with a small wooden cot in one corner and a wood-burning stove in the other. There were a kitchen table, three chairs, and a few plates and utensils scattered about.

"Oh, no!" Shaggy moaned. "Leave it to us to find the only cabin with no place to hide."

Just then, they heard someone pounding on the door.

"It's him!" Shaggy cried. "We're done for, Scoob!"

"Shaggy! Scooby!" a voice called. "Let us in!"

"Not by the hair on our chinny-chin-chins!" Shaggy replied. He and Scooby giggled.

"Come on, Shaggy, it's me, Fred," the voice said. "Daphne, Velma, and I heard you two screaming. Is everything okay?"

They stepped aside and let the others into the cabin.

"What happened to you two?" asked Daphne. "One minute Velma is showing us the newspaper she found, and the next thing we know you're screaming and running around the cabin."

"Scooby and I were eating the trail mix we found in the woods when that headless horror showed up and started chasing us," Shaggy explained.

"What trail mix?" asked Velma.

"Ris rail rix," Scooby said, showing her the bits remaining in his paw.

Daphne and Fred took a close look at it.

"That's not trail mix, Scooby," Daphne said. "That's horse feed."

"Rorse reed?" Scooby said. "Ruck!"

"But why would there be a pile of horse feed in the woods?" Fred wondered.

"Good question," Velma said. "But I'm more curious about where the headless horseman chased you."

"All the way around the cabin," Shaggy said.

"Let's go have a look," Fred said.

The gang went outside and explored

around the cabin. Daphne noticed the splatter marks on the cabin from the mud.

"It looks like a whole herd of horses came riding by here," she said.

"I'll say," Velma agreed.

Fred studied something on the ground near the water pump.

"Daphne? Velma? Come take a look at this," he called.

"What is it, Fred?" Daphne asked.

Fred pointed to a hoofprint in the mud. "Notice anything unusual about it?" he asked.

Velma and Daphne got a closer look and smiled.

"Judging by this hoofprint, I'd say our headless horseman has just galloped itself into a whole lot of trouble," Daphne said.

Fred and Velma smiled.

"Right, Daphne, and you know what that means," Fred said.

"It's time to set a trap!" Velma declared.

Chapter 8

"Here's my plan, gang," Fred said. "That headless horseman will come back for sure if it thinks the ground-breaking is going to continue."

"So all we have to do is stage a phony ceremony," Velma said.

"Right," Fred continued. "Shaggy, you and Scooby will stand in for Mr. Sturgeon and Happy Higgenbotham. When the horseman shows up, Scooby, get it to chase you into the cabin. Shaggy, you'll close the front door and hold it shut. Scooby, you run out the back door, and I'll slam it shut before the horseman can run out. We'll keep it trapped inside the cabin until Velma and Daphne return with help."

"Sounds like a great plan, Fred," Shaggy said. "Except for one thing."

"What's that?" asked Daphne.

"Scooby and I have had enough headless horsing around for one day," Shaggy replied.

"Right!" barked Scooby in agreement. "Ro rore readress rorseren."

"Are you sure about that, Scooby-Doo?" asked Velma.

"Rou ret," Scooby said.

"Then I guess you won't be needing this Scooby Snack," Velma continued. She tossed the Scooby Snack over her shoulder.

"Ro! Rait!" Scooby cried. He leaped through the air and caught the snack on his tongue just before it hit the ground. He swallowed it in a single gulp and licked his lips.

"Rummy!" he said. "Ret's ro!"

"That's the spirit, Scooby," Daphne said, smiling.

Fred picked up the two shovels that Happy and Walt Sturgeon had used before. He handed them to Shaggy and Scooby.

"Now wait until I get to the back of the cabin before you start," he said.

Velma, Fred, and Daphne walked away, leaving Shaggy and Scooby standing by themselves.

"Don't be nervous, Scooby," Shaggy said. "Just think about all those Chow 'n' Chew Chomper sandwiches we'll be eating when they finally build the restaurant."

"Rhow 'n' Rhew Romper," Scooby echoed. His tongue swept across his lips again.

As they stood there dreaming about all kinds of Chow 'n' Chew snacks, they didn't hear the sound of hoofbeats coming from the forest. By the time they looked up, it was too late. The headless horseman had burst through the trees and was galloping straight at them.

"Zoinks!" Shaggy cried. "Run, Scooby!"

"Right!" Scooby answered. He started running toward the parking area with the headless horseman in pursuit.

"No, Scooby! The other way!" Shaggy shouted. "Into the cabin! The cabin!"

"Roops!" Scooby barked. He abruptly stopped and turned around, running back toward the cabin. The headless horseman couldn't stop as fast and had trouble bringing

its horse around. Scooby ran into the cabin. The horseman rode its horse onto the porch and into the cabin after Scooby. Shaggy slammed the front door and stood in front of it.

"Let's go, Scooby!" Fred called. Scooby ran out the back door and helped Fred quickly slam it shut. Scooby breathed a sigh of relief.

"Nice work, Scooby," Fred said. "Now we've got nothing to worry about."

"That's what you think!" the headless horseman shouted from inside the cabin. A moment later, the horse and rider burst through the cabin's rear window.

"Rikes!" shouted Scooby.

The headless horseman pulled back its hood, revealing another greenish, glowing head. It reached up and lifted its head off its shoulders. Scooby crept backward, keeping his eyes on the horseman. His tail bumped into something. It was the water pump. Scooby jumped up and started pumping the handle.

The horseman laughed and prepared to toss its ghostly head right at Scooby-Doo. Suddenly, a plume of water shot out of the pump, drenching the horse and rider. The horse reared up and the headless horseman lost its grip. It fell to the ground with a loud *THUD!* Its greenish, glowing head landed with a *SPLAT!* right on top of it.

"Good work, Scooby!" Fred called. "You did it!"

Chapter 9

Shaggy came running around the side of the cabin with Walt Sturgeon and Happy Higgenbotham. They saw Scooby licking some of the lime-green deliciousness off the horseman's cloak.

"What's going on?" Walt asked.

"See, like, I told you," Shaggy said. "The headless horseman's getting its just desserts. Get it? Lime Jell-O? Desserts?" He giggled until he realized no one else was laughing with him.

"Get this dog off me!" the horseman cried.

"Hey, what happened to its voice?" asked Happy.

"Take a look for yourself," Fred said.

Scooby stepped aside as Happy walked over. Happy reached down and tugged off the horseman's head.

"Katie Kibble!" Happy exclaimed. "You're the headless horseman?"

"This time," Daphne said as she walked out of the forest. She was followed by Velma and Sadie Kibble. Sadie carried a large picnic cooler. Inside was another lime-green gelatin head.

"I can't believe those two sweet horse sisters were behind all this!" Walt said.

"Just as we suspected," Velma said.

"How on earth did you ever know?" asked Walt.

"Well, Mr. Sturgeon, it wasn't easy at first," Fred said. "We met a few people here whom we considered suspects. And when we found our first clue, it just confirmed our suspicions."

"After the headless horseman came by, we found a piece of the newspaper on a trail in the woods," Velma said. "And we remembered that all four of our suspects had the same newspaper with them."

"Aside from the Kibble sisters, who else was there?" asked Happy.

"Cullen Gasket, for one," Daphne said.

"Of course!" Happy said.

"And Rudy Rupper," she continued.

"It wasn't until the second clue that we were able to eliminate Mr. Gasket," Fred explained. "Shaggy and Scooby came upon a pile of horse feed in the forest."

"It looked like the same kind of feed that Sadie Kibble fed her horse when we met her," Velma said.

"And the same stuff that Rudy Rupper pulled out of his pocket, remember?" asked Daphne.

"Yes, yes, I do," Walt said. "But how did you know it was the Kibble sisters for sure?"

"Footprints," Velma said. "Or, to be more precise, hoofprints."

"Hoofprints?" asked Happy.

"When the horseman chased after Shaggy and Scooby before, the horse ran through the mud by the water pump," Daphne explained. "We saw the hoofprints, and then we remembered something the Kibble sisters had said about always being able to tell where their horses have been."

"That's when we realized the horse's shoes had the Kibble sisters' initials on them," Fred said. "We saw the letters *K-S-K* in the muddy

hoofprints. That left no doubt as to the horse-man's true identity."

"Amazing," Walt Sturgeon said.

"Why, Katie?" Happy asked. "How could you and Sadie do something like this?"

"We wanted to protect our horses from the noise and traffic a fast-food restaurant would bring," Katie said.

"Actually, it's not technically a fast-food restaurant," Walt interjected.

59

"But that's not all," Velma said. "Tell him, Ms. Kibble."

Sadie shook her head. "All right," she said. "We wanted to take over this land ourselves. We've been wanting to expand our horse farm for years. We figured that the headless horseman could put the kibosh on the restaurant and keep enough people away from the cabin that we'd be able to take it over without a problem."

"And we would have gotten away with it, too," Katie said. "But then you kids and your pesky pet showed up and ruined everything."

"Personally, I'm glad they did," Walt Sturgeon announced. "Because now we can go ahead with our plans. How about it, Happy, are you happy?"

"And I know it!" he replied, clapping his hands.

"I can't thank you kids enough," Walt said. "And you, too, Scooby. How can I ever show my appreciation?"

"How about a Chow 'n' Chew Chomper or two?" asked Shaggy.

"Shaggy!" Daphne scolded.

"That's all right." Walt chuckled. "I can do even better than that. How about free Chompers for life?"

"Rompers ror rife?" asked Scooby. "Scooby-Dooby Rhow 'n' Rhew!"

About the Author

As a boy, James Gelsey used to run home from school to watch the Scooby-Doo cartoons on television (only after finishing his homework). Today, he still enjoys watching them with his wife and two daughters. He also has a real dog named Scooby who loves nothing more than a good Scooby Snack!